Blood on the Dining-Room Floor

Zingu do you understand,

Of course she does.

Of course do you.

You could if you wanted

to but you always want

something else but not that

Blood on the Dining-Room Floor

Gertrude Stein

Edited with
an afterword by
John Herbert Gill

A Black Lizard Book from Creative Arts Book Company

m ·
12-86 gift 7.00

CREATIVE ARTS BOOKS
ARE PUBLISHED BY
DONALD S. ELLIS

For information contact:
Creative Arts Book Company
833 Bancroft Way
Berkeley, California 94710

Chapter
One

THEY HAD A COUNTRY HOUSE. A HOUSE IN THE
country is not the same as a country house. This was a country house.
They had had one servant, a woman. They had changed to two
servants, a man and woman that is to say husband and wife.

The first husband and wife were Italian. They had a queer way of
walking, she had a queer way of walking and she made noodles with
spinach which made them green. He in his way of walking stooped

and picked up sticks instead of chopping them and he dried the sticks on the stove and the fires did not burn.

The next ones were found on the side of a mountain. She had a queer way of walking, he didn't. She had been married before but perhaps not only then, at any rate she was soon very sick and is still in a hospital lying on a chair and will not live long. He was like a sheep. He was not at all silly. He was like a sailor. He had been a waiter. He cried when he was disappointed and fell down when he was angry.

The third pair came by train from a long distance and most unexpectedly they had a little child with them. She was a pretty child and went up stairs gracefully. He had been an accountant and loved automobiles and poetry. He was very quickly certain that a mistake had been made. She had lost one kidney and was soon to lose another. They wished all three to sleep under a tree but that is unbecoming and dangerous. There was fear and indignation everywhere until there was nothing any longer to fear. There never had been.

The next ones were immigrants. That is immigrants exist no longer because no nation accepts them. These however had been immigrants years ago when everybody wanted them. This is a pity. Not that they had been wanted but that they had been married after they had been wanted. At any rate she was wonderful with horses and he loved automobiles only he would never take a job where he would have to lie down under an automobile with his legs sticking out. This was distasteful to him. However that had nothing to do with it because he was to have nothing to do with automobiles. It must not be forgotten that it was a country house and so naturally there were visitors.

There were two visitors, not young, both women. What happened, nobody saw, but everybody knew. That is everybody knew except the two visitors. They only saw the result, that is they were only aware of a result.

Why should blood on the floor make anyone mad against automobiles and telephones and desks. Why.

This is what happened. There were dogs in the house but they were no bother. Listen carefully.

The next morning on coming to the desk to write a letter it was noticed that hair and dust had been scattered all over. This was not an accident and it was mentioned. Then some one went out to start a car. The owner of it naturally. It did not start. Then some one else went out to start another car. Once more naturally the owner of that one. The car did not start. Telephone to the garage in the town, they called out to some one else, the telephone is not working, was the answer. The telephone was not working that was a fact. There was another telephone nearby, of this fact as it happened no one in the house was aware except the person who telephoned to the garage. Soon two mechanics with two cars came. They found that one gasoline tank was filled with water and that the spark plugs of the other had been broken. The telephone man came and he found that a little wire had been detached and the piece of cotton that is wound around the wire had been screwed in instead. The mechanic spoke to the man servant at the request of the owner of the car, and said this could hardly happen by itself, and the man servant answered nothing. Just then more guests came and just then in the middle of everything there in the dining-room was a very sweet young man giving someone a very lovely painting. How had he come there, but that was not surprising, everybody knew him, but everybody thought everybody had quarrelled with him. Well anyway everybody kissed him and he left. The man servant served the lunch very well and then he and his wife were sent away. The garage man said send them away and forget them and this was done.

Lizzie do you understand.

After a while everybody went away that is to say nobody did stay who was not living there any way in the country house anyway.

These those that did stay and were living in the country house anyway, these had to go to a funeral right away. A funeral is always an event and this time everybody went that is to say only one went only one actually went because it had been a tragical event and everybody went. This was how they went and this was how they saw what they saw and no more.

Mind with her mind, she withered with her mind.

All please a face which smiled in case that she did mind.

For which if she did mind. She fell upon the pavement of cement in the court and broke her back but did not die nor did she know why. In five days she was dead.

Do you see what I mean. A country house is not the same as a house in a country and a hotel in the country is not the same as a hotel in a town but is it in a small town. A small town can and is near the house in the country which is a country house. They all went to the funeral. They passed up near the corpse, they kissed the cross they sprayed the censer and they passed near where they five of them, perhaps more, were standing. It was not terrible.

Find likely that she was dead.

In a hotel one cooks and the other looks at everything. That makes a man and wife.

Everybody knows all that. As that can keep everybody busy, nobody goes out. He did not go out because his mother had not, although his father had. He was like that. She his wife did not go out because she was the only wife he had. He said he did not want another even if she cried. He did not say he did not want another even if she tried and died.

Oh dear. We all cried. When we heard she was dead. Not that anybody minded. But they said. She is dead.

How did she die. Now I will try to tell. How she fell. And she was dead. Not at once. But in five days. Although many wanted to send flowers, in case, that she was, already dead.

How can she die if it is not right to die. In some countries nobody can die if it is not right to be dead. And if it happens in a country where nobody dies if it is not right to die, it is a dishonor, that if she is dead, she died.

In every country in some way it is not right to be dead, that is to die. And why. Each one knows why, in that country where no one should die in a way which it is not right to try.

Listen to this one.

Long ago, that is before this war, long ago, not so very long ago after all because she was not forty, but anyway some time ago there was a hotel-keeper who had succeeded his father, who had succeeded his father, who had already succeeded his father. In other words if there was to be a son and there came to be three, there would then have been six generations of hotel-keepers.

Six generations in some countries are not so many but still any way they are quite a few. It was the sixth who was not yet a hotel-keeper and perhaps never would be because he was to be a lawyer who said that there were six. But he became one, that is he became a hotel-keeper, and the reason why is this.

He was not yet a lawyer when his mother, yes it was his mother, it was she who was found dead, and not in her bed, not even dead anywhere.

It was she who was dead there where no one should be dead, when all is said, and very much is said, is always said.

And so he would not be a lawyer because, and this is natural, if a mother is dead, mysteriously dead, a son cannot be trusted as a lawyer, but he can be trusted as a cook, or as a brother of a cook, or as a son of a cook, or even later as a grandson and a father of a cook.

Do you really understand.

Way back before this war, there was a hotel-keeper, a very little man with very fine features and if he became very stout later he would be impressive, which he did, and which he was.

He saw a young girl who was also small but rather flat of face, who had a smile and who also later on would be stout but she would be stout and charming and be very steadily moving. She would be occupied with every little thing that she ever saw. She would know about clean linen, about peaches and little cakes, as few as possible of each, and yet always enough. She would oversee the maids at work, she would push them gently forward to do what there was to do and there was always all of that to do. For them and for her. All day and every day. She was always very nearly perfect when she stood. She never sat. Except when it was late and he and she would dine.

Think of all that.

Just think of all that.

He was little like his mother. His father had been and was tall.

All of us who think about it see what we see.

And then the war came, this late war. She had come from poorer people than he. He had not come from poor people at all. She had. This does make a difference and in a way does not make anybody glad. Does not make anybody glad.

When the war came he went away to the war. He was a little man and he went away to the war. Sometimes a little man does not go to the war, but he was a little man, and he went to the war, and what is more, he did not go and cook at the war, as many a cook did, he went to the war, and he fought in the war, and what is more, he fought all the long years of the war until there was no more war.

And all this time she was at home, home at the hotel. And was it home. In a way it was and in a way it was not, but any way it was the only home she had.

Every day and every day she had to see that everything came out from where it was put away and that everything again was put away. That was their way. That had always been their way. Any way was that way. Any way, she came that way to be that way. In that way she passed each day and each day passed away which was a night too.

Anybody knows that a night is not a day.

She cried when she tried but soon she did not try and so she did not cry. As a day was a day it came to be that way. But it was never only a day, and that a little left it to her still to cry, because it was a day, but it was not only a day. Every day had a day in its way.

In every day there was a day in the way. Do you think she tried. No she did not try because it always happened that way that the day was all day.

In this way one day she tried to find the night beside and when she tried to find the night beside, she cried. But she did not care to die. Of course not, and somebody knew but everybody did not know then. Just how she did everything. But it was very sweet and very feminine. And she did everything and her husband came home from the war and there were four children. This sounds different from the way it was. There were four children and they all looked like him, quite exactly like him. The four children were Etienne, John, Ernest, and Emily.

Now you see the family as it was and as it is only now it is no longer.

Now that he had come back from the war they grew richer and richer. Nothing changed but that.

They grew richer and richer. Nothing changed but that. After a war is over if they come back from the war and they grow richer and richer sometimes everything changes and sometimes nothing changes but that.

She had come from poor people and he had not. Nothing had changed about that. She was very gracious and smiled sweetly and every day everything was taken out and every day everything was put away; and sometimes several times during every day and sometimes very often during every day everything was taken out and everything was put away.

He was busy every day.

That is the way to see a thing, see it from the outside. That makes it clear that nobody is dead yet.

They grew richer and richer every day. The four children grew richer and richer in that way. They grew richer and richer. That was the only change every day. And every day the change was in that way. They grew richer and richer every day.

As I said they never went out and they never went away and they stayed that way they stayed where they stayed every day and they were richer and richer in every way every day.

One day he did not go away, but what happened. He was unfaithful to her. He never went away she never went away, they did not even go out a minute of the day any day, but he was unfaithful to her, and she knew that the night was a day. Just think of it. She knew that the night was a day.

Everybody knows in a way the difference between the night and the day. She did and she did not. He did but what difference does that make.

She tried to be while she cried. Oh dear yes. She tried and once when she tried, do you remember once when she tried she cried. She could not try and not cry. She could smile and take things in and take things out. But if she were to try she would be obliged to cry.

Lizzie do you understand.

Everything passed away except that they did get richer day by day.

This was all five years ago or so.

Now you see what there is to see. They are getting richer there every day. She is putting everything away and taking everything out every day and taking everything out and putting everything away as many times a day as there was time in the day.

What did you say. Yes they had somebody employed there who certainly did her share. She worked well and admired all there was to admire. And she gradually never came to be beloved. Her family

were well known too, and soon it will be very easy to see they had
nothing to do with it, nor had she.

All this was five years ago.

And now nothing happened. They were just as rich if only not
richer.

Their second boy the hotel-keeper's second boy was to be with
his father, he was to be with his mother and father, he was to be
there. And what happened. What often does happen. He was not
well and then he was to die. He is not dead. He did not die. But what
happened instead. A terrible thing happened instead. Somebody had
to be dead. The grandmother perhaps but that was no matter.

And then everybody knew it was true. She the mother fell out of
a window on the cement floor and then knew no more than anybody
what had happened before.

She was dead then five days after and everybody said the horticulturist's family said that she walked in her sleep. Did she walk in her
sleep. Had she walked in her sleep. Who had walked in her sleep.
Where did she walk. And whose was it that she walked. Whose was
it. Can anybody cry.

I wish to say all I know about the horticulturist who grew
flowers. They are a family of eight not counting the father and
mother nor any married brother. They did not belong in any way to
the hotel except that they had a sister who did, she was employed
there.

They said, that is, he said, he the horticulturist said, that the only
thing that kept the hotel going his sister was employed there were

three wills, his sister's will, the eldest son of the mother the wife of the hotel-keeper's will and the grandfather the father of the hotel-keeper's will.

Lizzie do you mind.

And now to tell and to tell very well very very well how the horticulturist family lived to tell everything, and they live in spite of everything, they live to tell everything.

Once upon a time there was a garden. It was an old garden and everybody who had ever been in it had been religious. In their way they had been religious. Even so there had been families. And this family as a history of the family had been famous. That is to say as the town knew about itself it learned to know about them. Not that in a way they were important. In a kind of way they were of no importance of no importance at all but they had come to be known to be of enough importance that they were important anywhere. As I said there were eight of them, four brothers and four sisters. The four sisters and three brothers exactly resembled the eldest brother and the mother. But of course this is not possible. It is foolish to think such a thing is possible since there was only two years difference between every brother and every sister until the youngest. And he was to be a priest.

It is of not the smallest importance what everybody knows about anybody's ways not of the smallest importance. In a way it does not make any difference even what is said. Not if it makes any difference anywhere.

The eldest of the eight sisters and brothers that is four brothers and four sisters was called the eldest. This too did not make any difference because everybody knew him and how important it was that nobody should know that they would think alike. At least they bowed alike. And so did she his mother who looked like him and wore a wig. Everybody knew she looked like him and wore a wig.

They lived in a garden and they lived off of the garden. They might be rich but as the family were like that nobody knew. If at any rate they suffered from poverty they had suffered long. This might make some of them intellectual. It certainly did this if they were poor.

They were not poor and proud. Nobody said that. Somebody said that they had too much manner but at any rate the elder brother was accomodating, he was ready to do anything that he could.

He had not placed his sisters where they worked. His brothers stayed at home and carried their garden with them wherever they went and none of them went very far but none of them stayed away and only one of them got married and he only had one child.

It was in this way that they lived and none of them died, not even the father who did not live in the garden, although he had.

She the sister who never left the hotel where she worked except to go home to the garden, which she did every day, was the eldest of seven that is she was younger than the eldest. And as such she felt herself.

Who was the hero of the garden and was there a father in this thing. There was but he disappeared. The hero was older than the seven, that is to say he was the eldest of eight, there were seven younger.

But to come back to the hotel as well.

Do any of you know a disease that makes complete black rings all around the eyes as if the rings were made with shoe black. The nursery governess of the little Emily had that.

Etienne who was to have been a lawyer, taking the place of his dead mother, stood at the door of the hotel, to meet the guests as they came in.

But to return to the garden and not at all to the same thing.

Once upon a time there was an eldest son the eldest of eight who had fought in this war.

That was not of any importance.

When there is a war everybody fights in this war. And if there is a war they all have fought in this war. Of course they have because in this way there is this war and not another war. The eldest brother once upon a time had fought in this war. Which they wish.

He had fought in this war, he would have been a priest before or after or during this war, but not at all. Nobody had died. A great many were killed but nobody had died.

Lizzie do you mind.

And so here he was and his brothers and sisters, here he was, and his mother, here he was. And a father. A father who lived alone, who owned and owned and lived alone, and had a cataract in one eye and nobody saw anybody cry but they worked all day too soon.

This is not a description of what they did because nobody saw them do it. Once the eldest brother with a watering can, a kind of apron on, and a watering can which he waved and between him and the one that came, was a man. Who was the man. A stout man, all the others were thin, a walking man, all the others bowed and ran. Who was this man, and he was in between.

I feel I do not know anything if I cry.

Slowly they could see their way.

Everybody proposes that nobody knows even if everybody knows.

There is no difference between knows and grows.

Gradually they changed the garden.

The eldest felt that he could not be a priest no not as long as his father was alive and his father did not die and later on the father did not die nor did they, not even a cousin died, but they got rid of the father just the same. At that time it was to everybody's shame so they thought, this that they had wrought.

By that time, the time that they had gotten rid of the father, how that could happen you will be told later. It was not a crime but a crime is in time. By that time it was too late for the oldest brother to be a priest and all the family wanted him to go away and pray very nearly right away after they had gotten rid of the father; the eldest brother, who had sent the father away. Every day another brother was there to say that he wished his brother to go away and pray. The next to the eldest brother could not pray because he was married any way. His wife had made flowers, artificial flowers, and now she had a child and they were all as glad.

Here there were no artificial flowers, they were natural flowers. Sometimes the flowers were too natural, they were wild flowers planted, which they sold.

When there are eight they never can become seven, if none of them die, and none of them can be put away. What did you say.

Could any place be shut away in time. To prevent crime.

Four three five. What.

Has everybody got it straight. So far we have two families and besides a country house.

We have three times crime.

Remember there was a country house where everything happened one day, and other things happened the other days.

Then there was a funeral.

Read the beginning again.

Then there was a hotel where something happened and everybody went, not away from the hotel, because nobody who just went and ate and slept at the hotel could know that anything had happened. It was wonderful the way they covered it up and went on. This was due to three strong wills, so the horticulturist said. The will of the hotel-keeper's father, the will of the hotel-keeper's oldest son who was not yet twenty and was studying to be a lawyer and the will of the horticulturist's sister who was employed there and who admired everybody, so she said, and was the one certainly helped to admire the hotel-keeper. A hotel-keeper needs admiring, because if he is a cook, he has to put forth a prodigious physical effort, particularly when he practically does it all alone and there are two hundred people in the restaurant.

Of course Lizzie you do understand of course you do.

There was nothing interesting in the horticulturist's sister's nature, she who was employed in the hotel, to anybody in the hotel. Of course not. This is all very well.

It was not she who said the hotel-keeper's wife who was not dead in bed but on the cement pavement instead, where she had fallen, walked in her sleep. No indeed it was not she. It was her elder brother.

Everybody remembers what I said about that elder brother. He was an elder brother with his mother and there were seven besides and nobody ever died. Not they. But this is not as it sounds. The youngest sister had not been nearly dead but sent away to stay so that she would not be dead that way. And she was not. She never was. She came back very well. And then later she went to a city to see the city and an automobile knocked her over, and a little spoiled her beauty, not that she was a beauty but she had had a fresh color.

At any rate everybody had liked to look at her. She was not the youngest of eight. She was the youngest girl and there was a brother who was younger. What became of him. He was to be a priest. To make up for the eldest one who wanted to be one. What had stopped him. Everything. The war. Poverty. Seven brothers and sisters with his mother and his father who was a stout man and who looked like a solemn man.

Do you remember what happened. The elder brother got rid of the father. And that was right. The father was using up everything and was getting fatter and the eight of them with a very bony mother who wore a wig, bowed and ran hither and thither and were not getting but were thinner.

This is the way they were.

The eldest brother, the brother and the mother and the seven younger did not get rid of the father. The eldest brother with the help of a rich old woman, not so rich but very old and very well known, and full of resolution and wonder got rid of the father. That is, the eldest brother following advice and taking his courage altogether got rid of the father.

And then what happened.

The father was safely away, the mother with the wig did not stay, that is she went another way, and there they were in the garden all getting richer and richer. Only it was not really richer, or perhaps nobody ever could be richer if they were really poor. Were they really poor. Ah alas. This nobody can know.

Anyway the sisters and the brothers, seven remember now, there were eight before, and they were all alive and as the brothers and the sisters thought the elder brother had done enough and now ought to go away and pray. That made them seven.

Now do you see this elder brother was only thirty-seven. Now at thirty-seven an elder brother ought not to go away and pray and naturally he did not wish to.

It was this elder brother who had said that the hotel-keeper's wife had walked in her sleep.

Had she.

I am sure I do not know.

Chapter
Two

NOW THIS IS ALL ABOUT THE OLD LADY WHO TREAT-ed the horticulturist the eldest of eight as if he were like herself.

Do you hear.

How many kinds of country houses are there, imagine, just imagine how many kinds of country houses there are.

There are many kinds of country houses, listen to all the many kinds of country houses there are.

This one had been one which was a small one. She who lived there now, she had not lived there when it had been a small one. Listen to her story. Anyhow listen to her story.

It is wonderful to be as strong when you are eighty as you will be when you are ninety, and as lively. I mean eighty and ninety years of age, of course.

This was she. She was as lively at eighty as some are at ninety, and she would be as lively at ninety as some are at eighty, and as rich. Was she rich, were her sons rich, and were her daughters-in-law rich or had they ever been. Daughters-in-law can be rich, if they ever have been, rich. But they were not rich, if they had ever been, if they had ever been.

There were two sons, one and one and one which makes three, but the second one was dead, it is very often that the second one is dead when there has been a war. And everybody knows, that there has been, a war.

So the two who were left did not look at all alike.

This is not strange if their mother is ninety and eighty and just the same as ever.

As I say she lived in the home that was big but she had not lived in the home that was big when she was young and the house was small. She had lived in another house that was about the same size as the house that was small. So her neighbors said. But this did not matter. She might have lived in either and her second husband made the small house bigger. By building.

Her eldest son was married, so was the younger one. The eldest one was married to some one who was not able to live continuously in a city as she had an absolute need for a private life. In between she stayed with her own mother, her own father and her own aunt. She might have married a rich man if her father had not lost his money in South America a long time before other people lost their money in South America. But she was well married and said a doctor had killed her aunt. She said this to the doctor's wife and to the mother of the husband of the doctor's daughter. And this even if it was true was insulting.

The second son was a rich man as long as it was rich to have a lot of money in everything, and then and alas and all of a sudden it was no longer rich, not any longer rich to have money, in everything. He had married a beautiful and young little girl and her name was Mabel. Mabel with her face against the pane looking out upon the rain. She had a little girl who was beautiful. But Mabel who had loved her old husband who was deaf and wore a monocle now that everything was not the same did not love him any more. If she could she would have gone to the bad. This is the history of Mabel.

And now whom did the old lady of eighty love. No one said she loved any one. But she did. Well she did not love any one but she loved to listen to the horticulturist, the eldest son.

And then she became poor.

She listened, she listened about everything and helped him to hear it. She helped him to hear everything. She heard everything, and she told everybody everything and this gave the eldest son the horticulturist's eldest son a great reputation. And her own sons did not mind. On the contrary they sympathized. And the daughter-in-laws. This is another matter and at any rate one that did not matter much as much as if it did that everybody thought alike.

About which they cry.

Oh dear about which they do cry.

Mabel had been kind to the horticulturist's younger sister and they all called her Mabel which seems strange and is not usually done.

You call the person you are kind to Mabel if her name is Mabel but the person who is kind is not called Mabel. Oh not at all. But to everybody's astonishment this time it was the other way around.

How confused are you all but I, I am not confused.

It really is not confusing.

How many houses and families do you know about now.

One two three four five.

And how many crimes.

One two three.

And how many possible crimes.

Six.

Chapter
Three

THIS BRINGS US UP TO MABEL AND TO BE FOLLOWED by the confessions of Mary M. in this case. There is no Mary M. in this case, but if there were this is what she would do.

Mary M. does not sound the same as Mary I. or even Mary D. or what is the difference between Mary B. and Mary C.

The confessions of Mary in this case.

I do in this case. Possibly for you in this case. I do in this case. Possibly not only possibly, but they will, possibly, be you.

This is what she said. I will remember everything that she said.

If you, possibly you, could conclude that I love best.

Mary said that she could not, not strangely not certainly not love best.

She also talked about dogs and mothers.

Do you remember way back in the beginning, when the guests were in the country house, and the servants were there there were dogs and they were said not to be any bother.

Mary said that this was not true. It could not be true. Dogs could not be anywhere and not be any bother because something always happened to dogs. And one loved dogs so. And if you did you thought of nothing else. This had not been true because a great many had thought of other things particularly then. Do you remember particularly then.

Mary said that in no case, just as much as if she liked, nobody could imagine or arrange it, there, where they were in affluence. She liked the word affluence. Nobody could be, not only, but really as rich as that.

Do you remember way back when the servants went mad, and the house was strange, and the young man was there and a great many said he was sweet, but he really was not. He was scotch and he had given it all away.

Please remember everybody's name. But nobody had given the names away. They never do when there is only a crime, that is to say a background for a crime. And you see the thing to remember is that when there is a background for a crime there is no crime. This is what Mary thought although she did not say, well you may say, she talked a great deal about a number of things, but what was most interesting was what she thought.

Do you realize how greatly everybody misses a little dog, at least they say they do, but perhaps not. This is what Mary said.

There is an adventure in what Mary said. There is always an adventure in what Mary said.

Mary spoke of Mabel but she did not know her. This was because we did not have time to introduce her.

Please prepare for Mary, for Mabel, and for many others. This is what Mary said.

Mary said prepare for Mabel, Mary and some others. It is just as you like.

Mary could be very venturesome and it always amounted to this. She had been well aware that it amounted to this. She was not afraid of sleep walking. Nobody had been who had ever walked in their sleep or heard about it. She had heard about the horticulturist's eldest son and she thought it was magnificent not to be ready to go away and pray, though it was just as much as magnificent. This is where Mary is cold.

She manages everything just as she is finishing the way they began. Oh please please Mary. This is not difficult as they are like that.

Now go on with Mary and make it exact and in detail from the beginning.

It is very early to begin with the end and so this will not be done. Oh leave anybody to be a son or a father of a son or a mother.

Prepare to cry as you try to be a son to a mother or a sister to a father or a brother to a mother or either of which you love best.

Chapter Four

IT IS VERY STRANGE HOW EVERYBODY OCCUPIES your time, very strange and very difficult and very hard and very much as it is.

It is not because they are not careful that you go away.

You like best everything that you do and you ask them to come and anybody can never ask them not to come.

It is one way to try to cry.

Leave this with this.

There is no difference between a very old woman and her son nor between the son and the son of some other one. They all live together even as they come and go.

Lizzie do you mind.

If a woman is an old one and remembers to like any one she is not an old woman and she does not remember to like any one.

This is not a crime.

But it can become one if after a while the one whom she remembers does not sleep at night.

Do you feel that this is right.

Remember I wish to tell you in every way what they do not say.

The horticulturist the eldest son did not sleep at night.

It was extraordinary how little sleep he had.

Gradually he slept less and less, so he said. It is always very difficult to know how much sleep is slept in bed. He said none. Everybody knew he did not sleep.

Now is there any connection between this and the fact that he had said that the hotel-keeper's wife she who had not died in her bed but on the cement walk instead had walked in her sleep.

Do you think knowing that he did not sleep would make him say what he said.

I personally do not think so.

I think it possible she did walk in her sleep.

I think in any case his saying this thing had no connection with his not sleeping. This came about quite naturally from the life he was leading and had led. No nobody was dead. Not in his family at any rate. Everybody knew that.

Why should they care. Mabel and Mary.

Mary disappeared.

By saying that Mary disappeared I mean that she left behind her a memory of her having been like Harriet, only Harriet did not think of dogs and Mary did.

How do you cry about a crime.

Mary had nothing to do with it and yet. She did disappear that is to say, if you wished, you knew where to find her. No one is anxious for breath or that.

Oh please play around fountains. No gardener says please play around fountains. Mary did not care about gardens either before or after she disappeared.

Mabel who never disappeared, she wished to go to the bad but how can you go to the bad if you have a mother-in-law who is as well as eighty years old and has never been other than just that. She the mother-in-law had always done just that, in short everything.

Oh Mabel Mabel cannot even fasten a pin, because she is so different in everything.

I often wonder if anybody knows how they manage to feel well. Well very well.

Why were they surprised to see her. Nobody ever is surprised to

see any one because after all there are a number of things. There are
servants, there are marriages, there are hotels, there are horticultur-
ists, there are butchers, there are other people living, there are
markets and there are garages and there are automobiles. Of course
there are and in each case it is all strange that they did not look upon
each other before. Before when.

Oh dear. Before then.

Think of it, think how near crime is, and how near crime is not
being here at all. Think of it. Think of it. Think how strange it is that
if they met they had never met. Oh dear, think of it.

Mabel when she was young and she still was young only now it
was not so, could make anybody think of anything. And she had
married, he was a large middle-aged man who wore a monocle and
she loved him. Her mother had been a beauty and her little baby was
beautiful.

He met her she met him.

Do you not see what I mean, nothing is surprising.

It was not any more surprising that he met her and she met him
and they were marrying.

It was surprising and the reason why is that the only thing that is
surprising is that there is a coincidental meeting. His mother who
was a person of distinction although a very old one was treating the
gardener's, do you see, a horticulturist is a gardener's, as if he were
everything. And the horticulturist's youngest sister had met Mabel

far away where she had been sent to stay, not Mabel, the horticulturist's younger sister. Mabel lived in that place there where they were
people of distinction.

Do you see, nothing is surprising but a coincidence. A fact is not
surprising, a coincidence is surprising and that is the reason that
crime is surprising. There is always a coincidence in crime.

There are so many ways in which there is no crime.

Chapter Five

AN ENTIRELY DIFFERENT MATTER IS THAT THIS FAMily knew another family. This also had to do with a marriage and everything that matters even orphans literally one orphan because the other one was dead before the orphaning was complete. In a way it never was complete because the mother was never dead, she was only completely put away.

There are several ways that mothers or fathers, mostly fathers and very often mothers are put away, even in families of distinction.

Now remember so far we have two we may say three.

The mother who was dead, well she was not put away.

The father who was neither dead nor put away, but they got rid of him.

And now the mother who was put away because she was really not what she should have been in her head, not she, she would never be dead.

All this is no suffering.

Nothing which happens is either prepared or not prepared, cooking, servants marrying or arranging.

Do you begin to see how here and there they are to be not where they were, although some are where they were, but others not.

A goat comes into this story too. Somewhere some one had two beautiful dogs that were big. One of them was a male and the other was a female, they were to have puppies, their owner, a woman, wealthy and careful too, always wore carpenter's trousers and carpenter's shirts and loved to work. She said when the puppies came there would be nine and they would need more milk than their mother had. She said this was always so. So she said she would buy a goat.

It is difficult to buy a goat, not that goats are really rare, not here and there.

She found through some one else a veterinary who could save lives, dogs' lives, cows' lives, sheeps' lives, and even goats' lives. Not so much horses' lives. This was because his father and his grand-father had been not veterinaries, he was not one either but he they she, even his sister always knew what to do. Other veterinaries were like doctors who saw everything through, but he knew what to do.

He was asked to find a goat a healthy goat. He did. And then. The horticulturist, the eldest son was asked to carry the goat in his car and he said no, not so. I will not have this goat go.

This really happened. The goat had been bought and paid for, and this often happened, so they said, whenever any one said, that the horticulturist had not said what he had said.

The goat had to be sold to somebody else and this too made every one entitled to say so, that the eldest of the eight may we call him Alexander was not any longer not only forbidding but forbidden.

Do you see how the whole place was ready, not for anybody to be dead but for anybody not to be interested in anything that was said.

As I was saying some one who was married, had been only seventeen. Three were married one, seventeen, one, sixteen, one, eighteen. These were all women of course and each one of them of a family of distinction. Each one of them married differently and they really did not know each other though each one knew who the other one was. Of course.

Alexander in a way met them all but not any one of them all knew better.

No horticulturist Alexander should be calling one of them Mabel of course not. Nor should he be doing everything for the other one, certainly not, or kissing the hand of the cousin of the third one, most certainly not.

The only thing that he should do was to say that the wife of the hotel-keeper had walked in her sleep. That was absolutely all he had a right to do.

There was the lady of eighty who liked to hear what he had to say and between them his father was sent away, not that the lady of eighty had anything to say, except that he was worthy of having this happen to him, he being so worthy, worthy of having his father induced to leave the garden to the rest of them and to go away.

The more you see the country the more you do not wonder why they shut the door. They never do in a way and yet if they did not it would be best.

There are many places where every one is married, even in the country, some of them are not. Think of it, even in the country, some of them are not.

Now we have come to the three young women who do not know each other and yet know who each other are, and they are each one married.

Mabel was married.

Helen was an orphan, that is to say her mother was put away and her father the major was killed in the war. You all remember the war. Some can forget a war. It is not necessary to remember or to forget a war.

a piano

Who remembers a door. Any one who remembers a door can remember a war.

He went to the war to be killed in the war because his wife was crazy. She behaved strangely when she went to church. She even behaved strangely when she did not. She played the piano and at the same time put cement between the keys so that they would not sound. You see how easy it is to have cement around.

I have often noticed how easy it is to have cement around because everywhere there are rocks and so everywhere if you have the necessary building and equipment you have cement. And in the country, it looks strange, it makes it look like dryness or like snow, like Russia or like sand, like a ruin or like a fog, oh dear some people like to live and look at it and some must, oh dear, stop when they see it, oh dear.

Do you see why I tell you about all this, it is because if you live in a country house you must know all this, of course you must, and you must come to stay, oh dear yes, you must come to stay.

Remember anyway it was not within a year but within three years that these three girls had married. I do not mind calling them girls nor calling them married, in any case except themselves and their marriage nobody was interested in them but everybody said as often as anybody could say that they were married.

Right right right left I had a good job and I left.

Chapter Six

A LITTLE COME THEY WHICH THEY CAN THEY WILL they can be married to a man, a young enough man an old man and a young enough man.

They did not know each other that is they knew about each other, that is they had seen each other and their families knew each other. Any families know each other know about each other of course yes.

A marriage is either in the winter or in the summer or even in the spring.

The spring one was one with a foreigner and the family never heard anybody win. Oh dear a foreigner.

They did not listen to him be a foreigner.

What did he do when he stood. He told that he was bold and it was horrible to be told that to be bold was to change money for gold. Think of how little they swim, how little a foreigner can and does and will and must and shall and favorably relieve leaving them for him.

There one married a foreigner, one married an old man and one married a soldier, can any one be a happy man and nobody notice them I wonder.

Anyway they all started to live in their way and Alexander the horticulturist knew their way and hoped some day that they would have a garden and he would do what he would for their garden. Of course he will. That is what happens in the country. Of course they will.

It makes no difference how often it is said that everybody everybody can go to bed.

That is the arrangement that they have made.

Alright. That is the arrangement that they have made.

Can you see crime. No not I. Because after all to live and die what makes them shy, nothing much, because they will have as much as they and and deny. Oh please try.

A dog can growl and that is not dangerous not at all it is not even annoying, no not at all. Because he is not angry, a dog is never angry neither is a cat, neither is a family neither is a gardener, neither is a

a piano

wife and child, neither is steadiness and suspicion and neither is chocolate or drink. For half as much. Neither is a railway crossing for half as much, neither is butter which I feel or oil which you feel or lard which they feel or mutton fat which they cannot feel. A dog has no countenance.

Now can I think how I will try.

You will say to me it has not happened and I will answer yes of course it has not happened and you will dream and I will dream and cream.

It has not happened. She slept and it has not happened. He will have been unhappy and it has not happened. They will be dogs dogs and it has not happened.

Shut forty more up and it has not happened.

Prepare sunsets and it has not happened.

Finally decry all arrangement and still, it has not happened.

This where I alone finish finally fairly well, I exchange it has not happened for it has not happened and it gives me peace of mind. Like that.

Any little thing pleases any one and in any way it is extraordinary in any way that at once of course in any way the whole thing has changed.

They said nothing happens in the country but there are more changes in a family in the country in five years than in a family in a city and this is natural. If nothing changed in the country there could not be butter and eggs. There have to be changes in the country, there had to be breaking up of families and killing of dogs and spoiling of sons and losing of daughters and killing of mothers and banishing of fathers. Of course there must in the country. And so this makes in the country everything happening in the country. Nothing happens in the city. Everything happens in the country. The city just tells what has happened in the country, it has already happened in the country.

Lizzie do you understand.

Chapter Seven

CERTAINLY YES DOES NOT MATTER CONSIDERABLY.
Anybody could be just as angry as pleased about Alexander.
Oh Alexander.

And yet Alexander, if not Alexander who can differ, or be poignantly fastened to alike.

Oh think it pleases.

Chapter Eight

JUST THE SAME IF THE PIANO IS PLAYED A LITTLE dog will bark. This has not given a name to Alexander, never.

Listen to all about Alexander.

And yet not one is interested in listening to all about Alexander and yet everybody is listening to all about Alexander. Think how curious this is. Nothing can be more curious than this.

But really the thing to do is to describe who came too.

Chapter Nine

AFTER THE MAN WHO TRIED TO PUT THE AUTOMO-
biles out of working order after he and his charming wife left,
nobody just then, but very soon more came. Who were they. He
looked as if he did not look like that. And she. She did. She was dirty.
A dirty man and a dirty woman and a dirty duck and a dirty swan and
a dirty goose and a dirty cow and a dirty apple tree and on account of
a distinctly cleanly row-boat. Oh why do you think all that they love
is the same.

Shall we be cherished as we think often and often.

They think theirs is allowed.

Now remember oh yes all remember that there came these two he who did not look the same and she who was a dirty woman. They stayed a month and just over. Of course they did. As servants. They would. Of course they would. They would be allowed. Of course they would. To go away. Of course they would be allowed to go away, most certainly of course, of course they would. Just why they would most certainly of course, of course they would. They would most certainly of course yes of course they would be allowed to go away.

Then next oh so young to be next.

If you think why they wish you will know, why they think, which they wish, that if, they were, so young, not so young, but as young, to be next. They were sixth.

But yes they were next.

Just now that is all of that.

Chapter Ten

JUST AS OFTEN THEY TALKED OF HER WHO WAS DEAD just as she died and they all cried. They still all cry.

They do, they know that she was there to try. If they were there. All who have done and died. Not only that but it could be, that if enough of a difference was made all which a difference as shade they were earnestly as shaded and they were if they were as paid. As well. As paid.

He her son may be thought to be thoughtful. Do not confuse the son of the hotel-keeper, she who was dead with the son the eldest horticulturist son Alexander. They had nothing to do with it. Listen to me, they have nothing to do with it.

Chapter Eleven

MARIUS TO MARIO I THINK EASILY.

Mario to Marius, and not to believe it at last, oh dear not to believe it at last.

Chapter Twelve

THIS MUCH I KNOW THAT WILLING TO SLEEP WILLING to make willing to see water may make a chain may make a lane between which they will not falter. But just when.

As I was saying meadows and grass are often dry in summer and if they are country houses, hotels are inhabited. In which case changes and pleasures are incessant but which makes it a pleasure to dearly love. I know how greatly a pleasure it is to dearly love.

The three who are married are as much married as ever and they miss themselves and their husbands quite as much and if for instance they do not like what they feel to be alike it is of course of no importance that their advantage is not easily taken. They are in place of not only wishing that they thought pleasantly of nearly and why they went as much and in as much as if in their manner they were not betrayed.

But are married women betrayed.

If they are married young that is to say if they are young when they are married and they remain young that is to say necessarily they are younger than their husbands who are older or very often not only older but twice as much older, in which case they plan but not one of them can come to know except that one that already knew the Alexander.

It is painful not to have the pleasure of prophecy in being uniquely a disadvantage, advantageous if they have refused to decline to know him.

Oh Lizzie do you understand.

Should they be briefly in tears a mother a cousin and no brother. How often does a young married woman who is not a widow not have a brother or never have had one. Uselessness can never mean next and by which time next is not only next but more than next.

Leave me and believe me.

Should it be a measure that they speak that they eat that they will declare that which they prepare.

Think if servants are inadequate if they are drunk if they are careless, if they destroy automobiles if they manage to help each other not only because they can but because neither of them can last out. Think of all this and then feel as well as ever being sure that there are more servants to be had. And if there are more servants to be had that is one thing. Nobody refuses fear. Not only themselves but for their dreams, because water as if it were a precipice in the moonlight may not disturb because of there being no origin in their dreams.

Those who do or those who do and do not do do not of course do not have it said of them that they do that they did do it. What, walk in their sleep for example.

Which one.

Which one oh which one. Walk in their sleep for example. For not at all. Usual is disuse.

Lizzie do Lizzie do try to understand.

How often could I add so many cases to as many more. But she said if I add will anybody hover as they do hover from cover to cover and so they shall be careless as she the old woman brought instead of a hare four little tiny chickens which might have come from a hen.

Not as strange as in case that there too somebody was killed only he did not die. Not for instance. If they are all secretly that is secret in shooting and one is shot, they will not die not officially of course not. This did not interest Alexander do you remember who was Alexander, of course you remember who was Alexander because he was not official. He of course and did constantly and did concern himself with himself and the other seven, he placed them where they could do the most good, to the other seven and themselves which made eight. The mother who had had the eight she had had a wig as having eight she could not resign to fly or die not by and by, oh sweetly oh said and not not why.

Alexander may be a witness.

*Chapter
Thirteen*

I FELT AS WELL AS WHEN I HEARD THAT HE HAD
trembled for a word.

Chapter
Fourteen

NOW IS THE TIME WHEN NO ONE KNOWS MORE
than in twos and threes. Say which you like.

Chapter Fifteen

VERY WELL SAID THEY CONTROL THEY MANAGE TO fasten they like what is very likely and they manage to exchange and they will be offered, three married women will be offered each separately because naturally there is no reason why any one would know any other one. As of course they do not.

So now you see. We have the triple theme, servants, yes of course servants, hotel, why there is always a hotel in every town by which you know who comes some say comes and goes but I do not I say comes.

Then also there are three young very young young married but which they mention. They may each have their mention their honorable mention their variegated mention their hope on their account. If one has a child not all of them have children. One and one. One of them has one and one of them has one and one of them has none not on their account.

And then next there is the horticultural garden and I give him the name of Alexander and he will not be intimate not with all of them particularly not with the subject of servants. No not at all. Young married women, well no not at all except and insofar that young married women are in a house and in that house is he and always welcome oh always welcome. On which account neither he nor she suffer.

And then there is the hotel, oh there he is never seen, nor has he been nor been ever seen. No there Alexander has never no never never been seen.

*Chapter
Sixteen*

DID I TELL OF THE THING I MEANT WHEN I SAID VERY
well.

Chapter Seventeen

MAY SHE BE A GRACIOUS MANY WHEN SHE USES THEY
have not known, where they were when they were alone.

And so in a way they say this way.

Think of this way.

One thinks of a change and for a change, for a change they feel
differently. And because of this it is a relief. And liking this they
confront massacre.

They have gone away ill-used.

Now think carefully of their ages, think. Think of replenishing also think. And think of the pleasure to the eye.

There is no doubt that if the young servant is better than an old servant he is pleasanter to the eye. The old servant is pleasanter to the eye when he is a very good servant. She also might be mentioned and this makes attenuation of crime. Do you remember what I said, there were one two three four five and now six couples who succeeded one another and anybody would know that something had happened but nothing had, not if anything had. Which they did. Ingrained which they did, but as well, which they did, more than, which they did, release and please and place which they did not do.

Of course that made it at no time that they had at any time they had at no time, any connection with a hotel. Of course they would not by which quite naturally not. Nor did they hear about it either although they were as nearly there. Of course not because to be sure they were occupied with themselves and their ways. Perhaps some and some did get put into the hospital some of them did know but even so they did not connect it at all with anything.

The matter is that they are accused but nobody mentions it. Once they are allowed to pass they are not alone not gone no one places one before the other. In time yes because they are all forgotten just as if they could have known each other which of course they did not do. That makes it all not a coincidence but a succession, do you remember that, who could be all in one and not remember that not only that. See here. Can one couple any couple who succeed each other the one after hears about the one the ones before but the ones before do not hear about the one or the ones after. Why not. Which does not interest them. That does not make mine fine. But just a reason. How any one can explain to any one how ours are around. Everybody knows but no one not any one is reason or in out is without motion who fell from eating anything. But then to cry. Think well to cry. How often louder out louder think well do oh think well to which in which well as well to cry. They might like theirs as just as just as well. They never knew that it will not last so last longer as so and so.

This again relieves a crime. Think of a crime, they are not based to please in time or scarcely. They should shade what they have. Come one come all, they are all gone. Believe me. And here we stay and once again we meet them, we meet them where they come. Such is our choice and such our chance, for which they welcome better than at all.

Did you hear me say they none of them knew anything more about this. Just think how they do not know anything more about this. They look worn but not with work but perhaps yes it is with work. Our work.

So they change none of them have gone none of them are at, a hotel. And why not, because there is no need of them there besides they had not thought of it. If they had it would have been a coincidence, but a succession is not a coincidence, and because this is so, oh yes, oh yes, oh yes I know, because oh yes I know this is so. Nothing happens. Is it likely that anything happens if nobody is with them in remembering.

Think clearly how often they venture not to forget.

There it is all here, that is all there is here of that.

And so dear woman she is dead, she the wife of the hotel-keeper and everybody knew where everybody went and what everybody did, and why everybody hoped and where everybody pleased and spoke and comforted and was answered.

And now when can I ask when I am answered. Which of course not. So not only there but here. If she the governess of the little girl passes she who had the strange disease which made black rings like shoe black around the eyes passes and looks very worn out everybody remembers which naturally they would do. Which is not strange as no one naturally forgets. But they can place what they place where they place. It.

Chapter
Eighteen

SO THEN THAT IS LIKE THAT. SO NOW FARTHER.

*Chapter
Ninteen*

TO SEE THE MARRIED BROTHER, WHO IS NOT THE elder brother but the only brother who is married of any brother or of any sister, pass is because he does not look like any brother or any sister, which are all of them together. And this is because he is married and so that is all there is of this. Will they put the elder brother, do you remember Alexander, away to pray. This one is not the same as that one, any day.

No and yes.

For instance if he induces any one to go on being good and they can use this, they any one of all of them, why are they not there, but really they could be cherished as each one of them are, one here one here as much, not one and one but one, and in this way it is not all over, no nothing is ever over even if they each one of each and every one are all over everywhere. Oh call out in your excitement.

One day there here was do not fear it was he who was there, he was called, yes I need him, that was his name, and all the same he did not only look like him, but like him. He said he had liked her, she the wife of the hotel-keeper who was dead, he said he liked her, and now it was all going slowly, but after all he she they all knew that that she had known how to be with her way of coming to have them stay. They did stay. For which she knew her way. He was a kind man and although he had a brother who was a farmer a sister-in-law who was a cripple and a mother and father who had been excellently what they were and had bought land just when they needed it, that is when the land needed it, and it was excellent. Excellent was its name.

And now, he had been there, when the lady fell, very well. Oh very well.

He had nothing to say of the three wills, the will of the grandfather, the will of the eldest son, the will of the sister of the horticulturist, Alexander, her name was not Alexandrine, as may be, not any one, can or cannot dream. For which, for sooth, for faith. Eat Eve when inclined. Her name, the name of the one who was dead was not Eve or Eva or just any name she had. Of course she had a name. There is no use in trying, if there is no use in crying.

He wrote to every one, he her husband wrote to every one, and he wrote beautifully, he her husband wrote so beautifully as he wrote to every one.

Can no one gather any one.

Chapter Twenty

AND AS HE NEVER HAD GONE OUT NOW HE HAD
to go out, he had to go out, he had to go out, to his dead wife, he had
to go out, to his mother, she was not dead yet, he had to go out to his
son the second son, he was not dead yet. He had to go out, he had not
gone out because he had never done any other thing than stay in.
And now he had to go out. Think of it not only he but he had to go
out and sometimes even to be out. Out is not out. Some in that place

can always be coming in and going out from staying in, but he not at all not at all not at all.

And now think about everything or which of everything. They will be will be will they will be they around. All of which tells.

Oh do not hesitate to try all of which tells.

Think well of which, may they be mention so, all or all of which of it tells.

Lizzie can it matter that you mind, if you mind it.

Alexander, of course, Alexander he was tall, they all looked as if they were all tall.

He asked and they went with him, strange if they had not been with him, strange women. But they all had a garden each one in each division each one had a garden and so it was never strange either at one or either at one time. Any one saying no could be known to come to be left out. Out of what. Out of nothing. Silly that you are.

Not any one could leave ingratiating. Not any one.

Just which they smile or orders which they smile.

Read while I write.

So many can say so.

Chapter
Twenty-One

ONCE UPON A TIME THEY BEGAN IT IS BEGUN.

Once upon a time a mother of six lost her husband and mourned him.

Once upon a time they were all in common they had it all in common that there were many although the town was small many families with many children.

This makes no success because success who shall who will who could who if they do. Nobody changes.

After awhile it is all known. Not three are changed for three. Neither or or either, or there.

Build away with neither as a guess.

There is no further guess. Everybody knows, and they need not say. That is why everybody talks and nobody says, because everybody sees, and everybody says they do. Not by and by, there are no secrets about what everybody knows and still they do complain. Why if why not why do they not complain. Not here not in not choice not and not we. We like ate and late not we.

And so it is often thrilled with a new one coming not thrilled for after all will they not stretch, not stretch to more but stretch to the same thing, at once they say, at once at which they call, they make no memory do for three.

It is almost at once why they call me as mine.

Think well of no danger that they will come or go away or no difference with which they last or no account for which in which arrange.

Lizzie do you understand.

Of course she does.

Of course do you.

You could if you wanted to but you always want something else but not that but not that yes.

Listen while I tell you all the time.

There was a country house in which they came to pay, nothing more than the rent. They of course paid servants' wages, sometimes twice, and anything else that fish and flesh and fowl and mushrooms can were needed. Naturally of course they did.

In case that a hotel should use words. It had no need because in spite of time, they came to please that all which held together was not their tender tie but always which they mean in which they cost. A hotel can all be had with which they want. For living and for leaving and for cost and taught. It is no matter so. Indeed and tall and all and small and well and fed and placed and bed. A bed is always comfortable if it is made so.

And then there were the rest. It has to be that holding all together, there must be a family whom nobody lost and nobody cost and nobody nobody which is nobody.

By that time they had not wished cake wished for cake.

Do you really understand, Edith and Lizzie do you do you really understand.

And they may carry meddle Mary Mabel medal. Oh do you see how aided to be by and by. Aided by aided by which they may not die.

Of course not rather.

Alexander.

Of course not rather.

Do you see how nicely a family is never three.

Six may not do.

Eight may do if nine is a mother. Should any one say anything farther.

In this in which no use.

And so the whole account in count and county. Forgive forget, forewarn foreclose foresee, for they may they be met to bait. He will add each strange lady to his past because they have a garden, hear me because they have a garden.

Each one may make a measure of the measuring that is worn.

They can apart from him.

His brothers may not say do go away and pray to him because it makes him angry not to stay. Which he does.

Do you understand anything.

How do we do.

Do you remember. It made its impression. Not only which they sew.

Thank you for anxiously.

No one is amiss after servants are changed.

Are they.

Finis

Afterword

In her long life, Gertrude Stein moved from obscurity to notoriety and a kind of fame. She was lionized and she was ridiculed. She made many friends among the creative aristocracy of five decades, and lost most of them along the way. During all that time she was writing, and it was as a writer she wanted to be known. Indeed, she came to believe that in the English literature of the twentieth century, she was "the only one."

Only once did she stop writing: In 1933, at the age of sixty she first experienced real success, with *The Autobiography of Alice B. Toklas*; after that everything fell apart, and she was unable to write a word.

The story of that summer of 1933, of how Gertrude Stein lost her way and found it again, is in microcosm the story of her life. For the rest of her years she would return to the task of writing about those months. But it was her first, major effort to tell that story which enabled her to break through her creative block and enter the richest period of her art. The chronicle of those days was her only detective novel, *Blood on the Dining-Room Floor*.

"It was a funny thing that summer. Things happened and they had nothing to do with me or writing. I have so often wanted to make a story of them a detective story of everything happening that summer and here I am trying to do it again."

The effort began as that summer ended, in the country house in Bilignin where the events had taken place. A three-day visit from the writer William Seabrook, a brilliant and deeply troubled man who shared many of Gertrude Stein's obsessions, was what enabled her to overcome the creative block: "it happened again, differently but it happened again." After six frightening months with no word in her that needed to be written, she was writing again. She had gone back to the routine she remembered from the Rue de Fleurus in the early days, when each lonely vigil produced what she and Alice Toklas called "the nightly miracle." Writing was not really something that she did. It was something that happened to her, like the visions of a Spanish saint, something that was given to you if you were a saint or a genius, synonymous terms in Gertrude Stein's personal vocabulary for those rare persons who spend most of their time sitting around doing nothing, "waiting for it to happen." This is how each night's writing was described: "It happened." Then before the rising sun could destroy the moment, Gertrude Stein would go to bed and sleep until noon or later. Alice would find the night's production waiting for her, and would copy it all out on the typewriter like a priest communicating a sybil's dark sayings.

Like much of Gertrude Stein's work, the detective novel she produced is a kind of interior monologue, in which past and present, the contents of the writer's mind as well as the room and the landscape in which she is situated at the moment of writing, are joined. The work comes alive if we read it slowly and aloud, and try to hear that rich, cultured voice (fortunately recorded during the American tour of 1934) speaking the words. The "continuous present" in which Gertrude Stein's writing lives erases all distinction between the work itself and the writer as she sets it down. Almost nothing is revised or rewritten; as the vision is given, so the vision stands, repetitions, false starts, contradictions and all. For whether she is writing an opera, a play, a detective story or a primer, it is all the same thing, the thing she called "Autobiography" in the full sense of the word's three roots: self, life, and writing.

"Can you see crime. No not I. Because after all to live and die,

what makes them shy, nothing much, because they will have as
much as then and deny. O please try."

It is in *Blood on the Dining-Room Floor* that Gertrude Stein
first uses "everybody" to refer to the narrator. She had never stopped
experimenting with ways to express the paradox of identity—that
everyone is the same and everyone is different. Gertrude Stein had
read through the Hebrew Scriptures and was astonished to find
nothing in them about immortality. But they had told of whole
nations and tribes and peoples as if they were single individuals. And
so she would go further, and tell the story of all of humanity by
telling the story of just one person: herself. She had written about
herself in the third person in *The Autobiography of Alice B. Toklas,*
where the author's identity is not revealed until the last sentence of
the book. Soon, she moved to a more outrageously literal level in the
sequel, which she would call *Everybody's Autobiography.* Eventually,
this quest for an asexual equivalent to "Everyman" would reach its
limit of absurdity in the novel *Ida:* "Everybody knew Ida, and by
everybody everybody means everybody." But it is here, in *Blood on
the Dining-Room Floor,* that this use of the word "everybody" to
refer to herself begins.

The difficulties which *Blood on the Dining-Room Floor* pres-
ents result not from the careless inattention which seems to charac-
terize much of Gertrude Stein's writing, but from an almost obses-
sive concentration on the task of writing:

*"Now can I think how I will try. You will say to me it has not
happened and I will answer yes of course it has not happened and
you will dream and I will dream and cream. It has not happened. She
slept and it has not happened. He will have been unhappy and it has
not happened. They will be dogs dogs and it has not happened. Shut
forty more up and it has not happened. Prepare sunsets and it has
not happened. Finally decry all arrangement and still, it has not
happened. This where I alone finish finally fairly well, I exchange it
has not happened for it has not happened and it gives me peace of
mind. Like that."*

We can almost hear the notebook snapping shut with a rueful
awareness of paradox. "It has not happened," which means that the
writing has not returned—this statement is made to contradict itself
by the very act of writing it down. And this gives her peace of mind.

In a magazine article called "Why I Like Detective Stories,"
Gertrude Stein put forth her theory that by getting the hero—that is,
the victim—out of the way at the beginning, the crime novel reflects
a peculiarly twentieth-century sensibility, unlike the romantic novel
which moves toward a heroic death at the end. In the same article,
she wrote about the problems she had encountered in writing *Blood
on the Dining-Room Floor.*

*"I tried to write one well not exactly write one because to try is to
cry but I did try to write one. It had a good name it was* Blood on the
Dining-Room Floor *and it all had to do with that but there was no*

corpse and the detecting was general, it was all very clear in my head but it did not get natural the trouble was that if it all happened and it all had happened then you had to mix it up with other things that had happened and after all a novel even if it is a detective story ought not to mix up what happened with what has happened, anything that has happened is exciting enough without any writing, tell it as often as you like but do not write it as a story. However I did write it, it was such a good detective story but nobody did any detecting except just conversation so after all it was not a detective story so finally I concluded that even though Edgar Wallace does almost write detective stories without anybody doing any detecting on the whole a detective story does have to have an ending and my detective story did not have any."

Why could her detective story have no ending? Why is there no detecting, even though clues and coincidences abound? It is because it is a story of crimes in which the guilty are not caught or punished. It is not "soothing" the way Gertrude Stein found most crime stories to be. These were true crimes, crimes that stayed in the memory because they were never solved; when there is a solution it is soothing but it is not interesting, we do not remember it. And so we find that page after page of her detective story summons the spectre of the patron saint of unsolved crimes in a kind of anguished litany: "Lizzie do you understand Lizzie do you mind."

The murder of Lizzie Borden's parents is the prototype of the kind of criminality Gertrude Stein was interested in. Her return to

America in 1934 provoked a number of reflections on criminality as part of the American identity:

"Everybody remembers a crime where nobody finds out anything about who did it and particularly where the person mixed up with it goes on living. I know I was perfectly astonished to know that even the present generation knew the name of Lizzie Borden and that she had gone on living."

The Fall River murders had taken place in 1892, when Gertrude and her brother Leo were living in Baltimore. Their father Daniel Stein had died the previous year, and there can be no doubt that they regarded his death as the beginning of their independent, creative lives. Her very first work, written while a student at Radcliffe, revealed what was to be a lifelong concern with oppressive fathers and with daughters who find revenge in parricide. In an article called "American Crimes and How They Matter," she writes about crimes in which there is no detecting and no ending to the story:

"There are two kinds of crimes that keep the imagination the crime hero and the crime mystery, all the other crimes everybody forgets as soon as they find out who did them."

She also writes about the notorious and also unsolved Hall-Mills murder case of the twenties, and how someone had remarked that Mrs. Mills by not telling anything "showed the integrity of the American woman." In developing this idea, Gertrude Stein seems to get the two cases confused:

"The case of Lizzie Borden is the same, she held back nothing

she never lied but she never told anybody anything that is integrity and is very American. The whole case was so American, the orchard was American, the surrounding family was American, the person who had the pig farm and had something to say but who never said anything, it was all so American, the causes which were there which were almost a poem and at the same time were filled with evil meaning and it was all so simple so evident so subtle and so open and nobody really came to know anything that is a kind of a crime that means something as an expression of the American character, yes if you know what I mean, yes it does if you know what I mean."

The language used here reflects an idiosyncracy of someone Alice Toklas once knew who always said "Lizzie do you know Lizzie what I mean," and links the "Lizzie" of the detective novel to Lizzie Borden.

The Borden case was memorable because it remained an unsolved mystery, which to Gertrude Stein made Lizzie Borden a "crime hero."

"And being a killer that is a natural killer and not a mean one nor one for any other thing than just being such a one that has always been an American thing and that has nothing to do with not being a good boy or a good son."

In order to follow the "plot" of *Blood on the Dining-Room Floor* it is necessary to look at other works in which the story is told in more detail, although a complete and consistent reconstruction appears impossible. The novel itself is difficult and labored, the

narrative is dreamlike, identities are confused. What is affirmed in
one chapter is denied in a later one, the writer's own struggle finally
prevails over the story she is trying to tell and the narrative line all
but disappears. A "Mabel" appears, and before we know it we are
back in the world of *The Making of Americans.* "The confessions of
Mary M. in this case. There is no Mary M. in this case. But if there
were this is what she would have said." The story of Mabel Linker
and Mary Maxworthing, names given to two Oakland dressmakers
whose story is one of the interesting parts of the early book, is
alluded to in this bizarre fashion.

In the Spring of 1933, Gertrude Stein and Alice Toklas were
living in the country house in Bilignin when the advances began to
arrive in payment for *The Autobiography of Alice B. Toklas.* They
immediately installed electricity and had a telephone put in. Kitchen
appliances were bought, even a bigger car. But the trouble came at
the same time. There was a series of unhappy experiences with
servants. After many arrivals and departures, they finally settled on
a man named Jean who had had a Polish wife. As the account unfolds
in *Everybody's Autobiography,* the title of the detective story which
grew out of the events in question flashes subliminally across the
page:

*"For some weeks nothing happened and then Janet Scudder [the
sculptor] announced that she was coming with a friend and that they
would stay a few days. Janet always has a friend anybody always has a
friend. As the earth is covered all over with people and they all do*

the same thing in the same way anybody can and does have a friend. So Janet and her friend were to come and they came later than they were expected, however they did come. They were very tired because I had told them to take two days to come and they had come in one. It is not a very long drive and still they had better not have come in one. Blood on the dining room floor and they had better not have come in one."

On the next day, they discover that Janet Scudder's car has been tampered with. Gertrude Stein tries to telephone the garage and finds that the telephone does not work. When she tries to go for help in her own new car she finds that it too has been sabotaged. There is total confusion.

"The Polish woman was there and I said well and she said yes and she said Jean is always like that when anything like that can happen. What I said. Blood on the dining room floor she said."

A message is sent, the garage man comes and confirms that both cars and the telephone have been deliberately damaged, and advises them to dismiss the servants, which they do. While all this is going on, young Sir Francis Rose—a painter of dubious gifts whom Gertrude Stein espoused for the last decades of her life—appears as if out of nowhere with a painting, apparently a peace offering. He, too, has a friend, but in this case the friend is totally out of favor and must remain outside in the car. This part of the story figures interestingly in the first part of *Blood on the Dining-Room Floor:*

*"Just then more guests came and just then in the middle of
everything there in the dining-room was a very sweet young man
giving someone a very lovely painting. How had he come there, but
that was not surprising, everybody knew him, but everybody thought
everybody had quarrelled with him. Well anyway everybody kissed
him and he left."*

In the third chapter of the novel there is a curious turnabout:

*"Do you remember way back when the servants went mad and
the house was strange, and the young man was there and a great
many said he was sweet, but he really was not. He was scotch and he
had given it all away. Please remember everybody's name. But
nobody had given the names away. They never do when there is only
a crime, that is to say a background for a crime. And you see the thing
to remember is that when there is a background for a crime there is
no crime."*

Later that summer, the next "crime" occurs. In nearby Belley, a
Madame Pernollet is found sprawled on the cement courtyard of her
husband's hotel. Five days later she is dead.

Pernollet was a fifth-generation hotel-keeper. His wife had
helped him, they had worked hard over the years and never went
anywhere, never left the hotel. When he returned from the war, they
had four children. The oldest son was going to be a lawyer, the
second was to follow in the hotel business. And then, Gertrude Stein
tells us, Madame Pernollet's husband was unfaithful to her, right

there in the hotel where they lived and worked. Things went on as before, but Madame Pernollet was noticeably unhappy and preoccupied. And then she was dead.

Was it an accident? Suicide? Murder? What worried Gertrude Stein was that a certain young man she called "Alexander" in her novel, a horticulturist, had put it about that Madame Pernollet walked in her sleep, as if he needed to provide an explanation for the tragedy. His story was accepted, the verdict was accidental death: "It is interesting how they covered everything up and went on." But it was Alexander's own sister who had been working at the hotel, being "very helpful in everything," at the time of Pernollet's infidelity. There is more than a hint that brother and sister had a plot to get the wife out of the way so that the younger woman could secure a solid position in the prosperous Pernollet business. Alexander was known to have gotten rid of his own father and taken over the family horticulture business himself.

Of all the happenings of that unnatural summer, the story of a Madame Caesar and an English woman who occasionally lived with her seems the most promising material for a detective story. But although the characters are introduced in *Blood on the Dining-Room Floor* the story is never told and the crime is not mentioned at all. We find it in *Everybody's Autobiography* and, in another version, in the short piece called "A Waterfall and a Piano" which concludes as follows:

*"The Englishwoman came back. She was very cheerful and had
seen all her friends and had plans for the nine puppies and the rest of
the garden. Then the dogs found her. She had put her cap beside her
and there were two bullets in her head and she was dead. The police
disturbed her they had no business to, the protestant pastor buried
her he had no business to, because nobody had been told what had
happened to her. The doctor said nobody could shoot themselves
twice. All the doctors said that. An officer said that this was not so.
During the wars when an officer wanted to be dead he often put a
bullet into his head. But it was very often true, that he did not succeed
in doing more than putting a bullet into his scalp and then he sent a
second one after. . . . And every one still talks about it all but not so
much now as they did. An American comes to visit in place of the
Englishwoman but she has not come to be dead."*

This is a good, *frisson*-inducing ending. Clearly the American
woman's days are numbered.

In *Everybody's Autobiography,* the ending is different. One of
the local citizens, worried about what is going on, telephones Gertrude Stein to come at once when the body is discovered. But when
she arrives at the scene of the crime, the body has been taken away,
and clearly no one is interested in getting at the truth. She and her
friend Bernard Faÿ, who is visiting at the time, go to Madame
Caesar's house and find an uneasy gathering:

"There was an American woman there who knew all about

Benjamin Franklin . . . and outside there were two the man who puts in electric heaters"—like Gertrude Stein, Madame Caesar had that summer put in electricity—*"and his wife, and inside there was a very large woman who was not moving and she was all in black as if it might be evening. She was the mother of the wife of the electrical installer and later she stayed there altogether."*

Gertrude Stein and Alice Toklas had been friendly with Madame Caesar and her circle but after the unexplained death this comes to an end:

"Anyway it was only once that we saw Madame Caesar, she came to see us and those who wanted to see her were there and in a little while any one was frightened of her and about her and then in a little while although she was always there nobody was there with her that is to say Mrs. Steiner never was there any more and the wife of the electric installer was."

It is odd what Gertrude Stein concludes about the whole affair:

"It never bothered us any more but every time I want to write I want to write about what happened to her. Anyway there is no use in not forgetting what you know and we do not know what happened to her."

People visiting Gertrude Stein at Bilignin were surprised to find that French people in the country locked their houses and even built walls around them. It was the typical American notion that crimes only take place in big cities.

"They said nothing happens in the country but there are more changes in a family in the country in five years than in a family in a city and that is natural. If nothing changed in the country there could not be butter and eggs. There have to be changes in the country, there had to be breaking up of families and killing of dogs and spoiling of sons and losing of daughters and killing of mothers and banishing of fathers. Of course there must in the country. And so this makes in the country everything happening in the country. Nothing happens in the city. Everything happens in the country. The city just tells what has happened in the country, it has already happened in the country. Lizzie do you understand."

Blood on the Dining-Room Floor comes to an end but, as Gertrude Stein herself said of it, it has no ending. There is a final chapter which begins "Once upon a time they began it is begun." Like the curtain line of Eliot's *The Cocktail Party,* the ending of this detective story marks a new beginning, so nothing more has to be said. "There is no further guess. Everybody knows, and they need not say. That is why everybody talks and nobody says, because everybody sees, and everybody says they do. Not by and by, there are no secrets about what everybody knows and still they do complain." There is a final cacophony of words, a recapitulation of words and names and phrases, and the insistent question is repeated, this time with a new name added:

"Lizzie do you understand. Of course she does. Of course do you.

You could if you wanted to but you always want something else but not that but not that yes . . . . Do you really understand, Edith and Lizzie do you do you really understand."

If there was anyone who belonged in the company of Lizzie Borden and the writer herself, it was Gertrude Stein's sometime friend, confidante and rival, Edith Sitwell, whose girlhood, indeed whose entire life had been made a hell of physical and psychological torment by a father whose cruelty to her bordered on insanity.

The detective story comes to an end, and with it a season of fear and pain. "We quieted down and I began working and naturally I began writing lectures to be given, as if we were going to America . . . . When I begin writing them I gave up thinking about anything. What is the use of thinking about anything and then our ordinary way went on."

Blood on the Dining-Room Floor was published two years after Gertrude Stein's death. The text was edited by Donald Gallup, and the handsome limited edition was created by the Banyan Press. Alice B. Toklas wrote to Claude Fredericks and Milton Saul (she called them the "Banyan Tots") of the pleasure their "perfect book" would have given its author: "she would have said that the text and its presentation were equally good." A few years later, in a chapter of her famous cookbook called "Murder in the Kitchen" Alice Toklas would remember how she and Gertrude Stein had first become interested in detective stories as typical of the twentieth century way of viewing life. She tells of her own murders: first a carp (a bloody deed with a knife) then six lovely doves, strangled with her bare hands while Gertrude Stein was out because she "did not like to see work being done." And she concludes of this ordeal:

"It was a most unpleasant experience, though as I laid out one by one the sweet young corpses there was no denying one could become accustomed to murdering."

Bibliographical Note

The events of 1933 are described in two short pieces, "Is Dead" and "A Waterfall and a Piano," contained in *How Writing Is Written,* edited by Robert Bartlett Haas (Santa Barbara, Black Sparrow Press, 1977). "American Crimes and How They Matter" and "Why I Like Detective Stories" may be found in the same volume.

William Seabrook tells his own story of his 1933 visit to Bilignin in his autobiography *No Hiding Place* (Philadelphia, Lippincott, 1942). Marjorie Worthington gives her version in *The Strange World of Willie Seabrook* (New York, Harcourt, Brace and World, 1966).

Sir Francis Rose, in a bizarre autobiography called *Saying Life* (London, Cassell, 1961) which is dedicated to Gertrude Stein, informs us that she had always wanted to write a detective story called *Blood on the Dining-Room Floor* but had never gotten around to it. He does tell of that visit when he gave Gertrude Stein the painting and she kissed him, but alludes to the death of Madame Pernollet as if it had happened many years later when he visited Bilignin after the war.

The primary autobiographical source for the period in question is Gertrude Stein's *Everybody's Autobiography,* (New York, Random House, 1937).

—John Herbert Gill

About the Editor

John Herbert Gill is a graduate of Yale University, where he studied with Donald Gallup, the distinguished bibliographer who has played such an important role in preserving Gertrude Stein's literary legacy. Father Gill has published numerous articles and reviews, mostly in the area of education and public policy. He is presently a priest of the Episcopal Church in the Diocese of Long Island.